SCARUM FAIR

POEMS BY
JESSICA SWAIM

ILLUSTRATIONS BY
CAROL ASHLEY

WORDSONG

HONESDALE, PENNSYLVANIA

For Cathy Partusch, a frightfully good friend
—*J.S.*

To my brave little boy, Ryan . . . Don't let
anything scare you. Special thanks, Mickey,
for all your support.
—*C.A.*

Text copyright © 2010 by Jessica Swaim
Illustrations copyright © 2010 by Carol Ashley

Wordsong
An Imprint of Boyds Mills Press, Inc.
815 Church Street
Honesdale, Pennsylvania 18431
Printed in the United States of America

Library of Congress Cataloging-in-Publication Data

Swaim, Jessica.
  Scarum fair / by Jessica Swaim ; illustrations by Carol
Ashley. — 1st ed.
     p. cm.
  ISBN 978-1-59078-590-4 (hardcover : alk. paper)
 1. Carnivals—Juvenile poetry. 2. Ghouls and ogres—
Juvenile poetry. 3. Children's poetry, American.
 4. Humorous poetry, American. I. Ashley, Carol, ill. II. Title.
  PS3619.W345S33 2010
  811'.6—dc22
                              2008040336

First edition
The text of this book is set in 14-point Minion Pro.
The illustrations are done in acrylics, graphite,
and pen and ink.

10 9 8 7 6 5 4 3 2 1

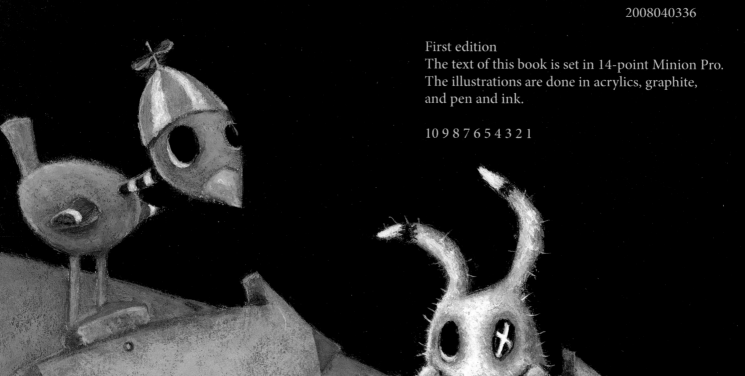

CONTENTS

THE GHOUL AT THE GATE

Hey, kid,
it's almost midnight,
and these woods are dark and deep.
What are you doing way out here?
Why aren't you home, asleep?

Turn back,
or you'll regret it.
See that sign up on the gate?
What if The Hand should pull you in?
What if . . . Oh no! Too late!

4

CARNIVAL CREEPS

Welcome NOT
to Scarum Fair!
The Hand will point
you here and there.
Or flip a coin
to help you choose.
Heads or tails,
you're bound to lose.

DOWN

HERE

UP

THERE

DEADBEATS

Let's all give a hand to the Sleeping Dead Band,
with the flutist who toots as he dozes.
The ghost on bassoon plays a sad, haunting tune,
while the ghoul on the sax de-composes.

THE TATTOO ARTIST

He's known for flashy colors
and for sinister designs.

You close your eyes and shudder
while he inks in all the lines.

He tells you that his work is done,
and then you burst out bawling.

Your bug tattoos have come alive,
and now your skin is crawling!

DR. CRUNCH

Does your cranium feel creaky?
Is your spinal column bent?
Well, have a seat in
Dr. Crunch's Chiropractic Tent!

He'll pulverize your sternum,
and he'll disconnect your knee,
then move your metatarsals
where your tailbone used to be.

He'll reconstruct your rib cage
and attach it to your shin,
then give your sacroiliac
a jaunty little spin.

Take it from the Hunchback,
(still adjusting to his hunch),
you'll never get a lucky break
from twisted Dr. Crunch.

POULTRYGEIST

There's no other critter
so fowl at the fair
as the ghostly red chicken
who flies through the air,
dropping her eggs
with im-*peck*-able aim,
making you sorry
that you ever came.
Down the back of your neck
runs gelatinous goo.
"Tough cluck!" the hen cackles.
"The yolk is on *you*!"

SCRAMBLED EGGS

The incubator holds a lot
of odd, misshapen eggs.
Two scaly heads poke out of one,
then come the feet and legs.
Life is tough. It's hard enough
for reptile kids to hatch.
Who says that their assorted parts
are all supposed to match?

11

Have some devil's food cake.
What a sizzling delight!
With a tiny red pitchfork,
you'll savor each bite
till your tongue catches fire
and your breath turns to steam,
then you'll cool yourself off
with a bowl of I-Scream.

Devil's Food

CAKE

I-SCREAM

Step right up and get your cone!
One scoop will chill you to the bone!
It's made with ears of Arctic hare
and topped with chopped-up polar bear
with just a pinch of penguin beak
to numb your throat
so you can't speak.

Your kneecaps shake,
your nose turns blue,
your lips take on a purplish hue,
your liver gels by slow degrees,
your thumbs go numb, your tonsils freeze—
a bitter fate, but here's the sting:
the crows will thaw you out next spring.

THE PALM READER

Madame Ratowski addresses The Hand.
"I see in your future a gold wedding band.
A fortune will slip through your fingers, I fear,
when you lose a big poker game later this year.

"Your garden will die," Madame says with a frown.
"You could have a green thumb if you'd just knuckle down."
She closes The Hand, and she gives it a squeeze.
"You owe me ten bucks and a slice of swiss cheese."

The Hand waves good-bye as it exits the booth
with a fistful of lies and a pinch of the truth.

CAT-HAIR STEW

Witch Helen makes a special brew
which, truth be told, is cat-hair stew.
She seasons it with smelly spice,
with rotting fish, and moldy mice,
then stirs it with a hickory stick
to form a paste that's extra-thick.
She serves it in a fur-lined cup
and waits until you cough it up,
then plops it back to make more brew . . .
the same old, same old cat-hair stew.

15

PUMPKIN BOWLING

Hey, guys and ghouls,
it's time to bowl!
Let's see those jack-o'-lanterns roll!
Throw a strike or make a spare,
pumpkin guts go everywhere.
Oh, my golly—oh, my gosh,
aren't you glad you're not a squash?

16

COFFIN RACE

There's no need to have a license.
There's no need to be alive.
The competition's stiff tonight,
'cause dead folks love to drive!

You'll see expensive models
plus some long-forgotten makes.
Reclining seats are optional,
but not a soul needs brakes.

The racetrack spirals downward
to the finish, and no wonder:
the winner gets a floral wreath
and parking six feet under.

THE ODD COUPLE

The Head and The Hand,
what a frightening pair!
They've fought tooth and claw
since they came to the fair.

She flattened his hat,
then he chewed up her glove.
It was no time at all
before push came to shove.

Now they both need a break,
so they grab a quick lunch.
The Head has I-Scream
while The Hand sneaks a . . . PUNCH!

The Werewolves' Den

Are you sick from too much I-Scream?
Is the carnival too loud?
Then curl up in our den awhile,
escape the raucous crowd.

If you'll come a little closer,
we will nibble on your nose,
we'll lick your hands, your face, your ears,
your scrumptious little toes.

Like our friendly canine cousins,
we're a cute and cuddly bunch.
Just think of us as puppies,
and we'll think of you as . . . lunch.

POISON DART FROG

Witch Clara has a tiny frog
that plays the cruelest joke
on creeps who try to capture him,
'cause they're the ones who croak.

HEAD LOUSE

This tiny pest
requires no care.
She's happy strolling
through your hair
and laying eggs
that quickly hatch.
So every day
you start from scratch.

HUNGRY BUZZARD

Rotting flesh is what he needs
to help him grow and thrive,
so when the buzzard comes to call,
it's best to look alive.

PUNCH, ANYONE?

The vampires all cheer,
for Count Dracula's here
with three bowls labeled A, B, and O.
One vamp grabs a cup,
tells the Count, "Fill 'er up!"
then he samples three pints in a row.

"Type A's rich and red, and the taste
knocks me dead," says the vamp,
"though I doubt it's nutritious.
Type B is so thick
it makes me feel sick,
but type O's positive-ly delicious!"

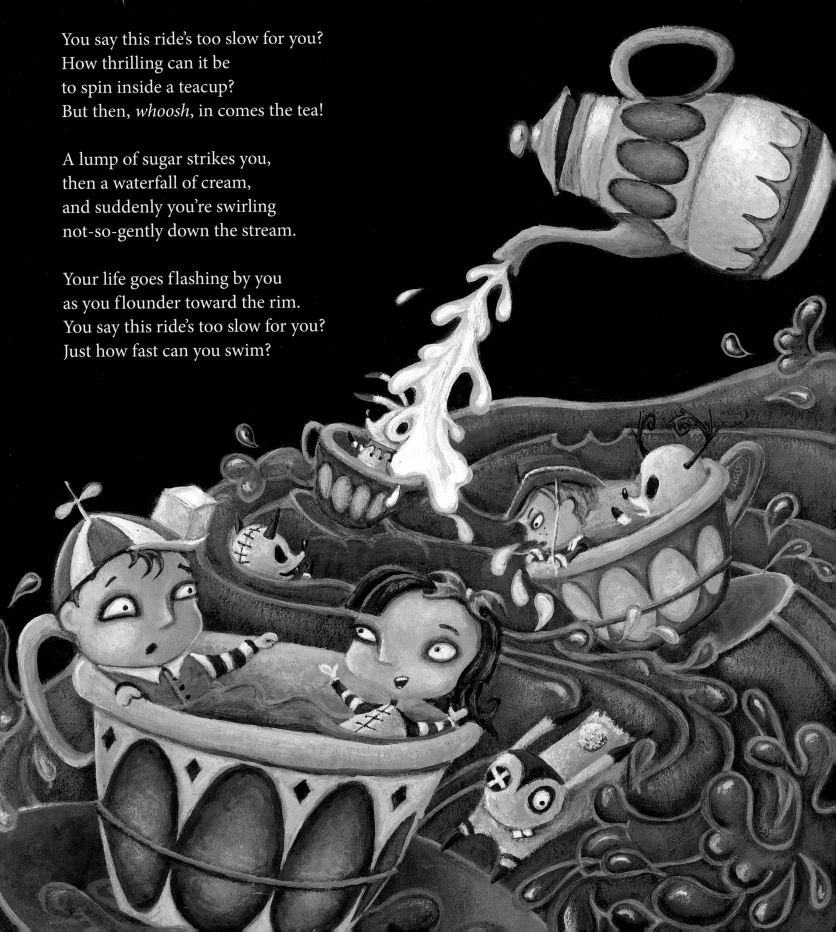

TEACUP TERROR

You say this ride's too slow for you?
How thrilling can it be
to spin inside a teacup?
But then, *whoosh*, in comes the tea!

A lump of sugar strikes you,
then a waterfall of cream,
and suddenly you're swirling
not-so-gently down the stream.

Your life goes flashing by you
as you flounder toward the rim.
You say this ride's too slow for you?
Just how fast can you swim?

THE SCARY-GO-ROUND

Come take a ride on the Scary-Go-Round,
two hundred forty-three feet off the ground,
with dragons and werewolves and one rabid hound
that nip at your heels as they chase you around.

Over and over, from midnight till noon,
you're forced to keep time to the same tinny tune
while the Christmases come and the Halloweens go,
you race through the rain and you slog through the snow,
which freezes your eyebrows and whitens your face,
yet still you must run at the same manic pace.

Muster a smile as you wave to your friends
from the Scary-Go-Round,
where the fun never ends . . .

MUMMY WRAP

You'll dig this classic, timeless style
that thrived along the river Nile—
a comfy wrap for day and night
in royal blue or tombstone white.
It hugs your bones and calms your nerves,
accentuates your shapely curves,
accommodates most every size
with buttons, snaps, or lasting ties.
It will not chafe, it will not bind,
so rest in peace. Relax! Unwind!

FREAKY FASHION SHOW

25

HAND-KNIT MITT

All Hand-knit, the Giggle Mitt
consists of wiggly stuff
like lizard tails and cobra tongues
and caterpillar fluff.
Fits most adults and gives results
that moms and dads are after:
make the kiddies tickled pink,
then watch 'em die of laughter!

SHROUD SALE

This spooky Hand-embroidered shroud
is sure to stun the graveyard crowd.
Won't shrink or stretch. Won't fade or tear.
No need to iron, just wash and wear.
Comes in linen, lace, or vinyl.
No returns, all sales are final!

VAMPIRE WEDDING GOWN

She will tickle the town
in this cobwebby gown
of imported tarantula lace,
with a necklace of rats
and a bracelet of bats
and a poisonous smile on her face.

She will float down the aisle,
Transylvania-style,
in her stockings with centipede seams.
At midnight she'll marry.
Oh, isn't she scary?—
the ghoul of Count Dracula's dreams!

COUNT DRACULA'S WEDDING

The Count and his girl,
who's as pale as a pearl,
make a perfectly hideous pair.

For years they've gone steady.
At last they are ready
to marry right here at the fair.

The gargoyles grin
as the crowd shuffles in
to the candlelit Chapel of Gloom.

The bride's creepy cousins
are followed by dozens
of bloodthirsty friends of the groom.

When she gives him her heart,
until death do them part,
evil spirits dissolve into laughter.

The moon's full tonight,
and she's yummy to bite.
Won't their life be a scream ever after?

RATTLER COASTER

You're bound to recognize her
by the pattern on her back
and the buzzing of her rattles
as she slithers down the track.
The oldest living member
of a species no one likes,
she puts the "scare" in Scarum Fair,
where bad luck often strikes.

A SNAP DECISION

It's time to go, so you pick one last ride.
You climb to the top of the Crocodile Slide
and land at the bottom, in Thrash-a-Lot Lake,
with others who've made the same stupid mistake.

"Croc, let me go!" you repeatedly shout
as you spit in his eye and you bang on his snout.
But you've already paid, and it's too late to beg.
The Crocodile Slide costs an arm and a leg.

THE GHOUL SAYS GOOD-BYE

Hey, kid,
it's almost morning,
and your face looks kinda green.
I bet your stomach's churning
from the spooky stuff you've seen.

I told you
not to come here.
Did you listen to me? No!
You'll never leave the Scarum Fair.
The Hand won't let you go . . .